CLARA CLAUS
saves
Easter

Praise for the Clara Claus Series

"A charming story that should be inside every Christmas stocking"
Laura Ellen Anderson,
author of *Amelia Fang* and *Rainbow Grey*

"The perfect book to share with young believers at Christmas time. I loved it!"
Jen Carney,
author of *The Accidental Diary of B.U.G.*

"This brilliant book is going to be the best thing since sliced (ginger)bread."
Louise Gooding, author of *Just Like Me*

"A fantastically, festive tale that is bound to delight and entertain young readers."
Booklover Jo

"What a brilliant Christmas story, we loved it."
Karen's World Blog

"Break out the candy canes and sugar cookies! Christmas spirit runs through every line..."
Scope for Imagination Blog

"Full of festive fun... the perfect stocking filler."
WRD magazine

CLARA CLAUS
saves
Easter

Bonnie Bridgman

Illustrated by **Louise Forshaw**

TINY TREE
CHILDREN'S BOOKS

TINY TREE
CHILDREN'S BOOKS

First Published 2022
Tiny Tree Children's Books
(an imprint of Matthew James Publishing Ltd)
Unit 46, Goyt Mill, Marple, Stockport SK6 7HX

www.tinytreebooks.com

ISBN: 978-1-913230-39-5

To my Robins who will always
be my little bunnies - B.B

For my Mam - L.F

CHAPTER ONE

Help!

'Clara!' Jingles' voice was high and screechy as he came bounding into the stables.

Clara Claus bolted upright at the elf's urgent tone, and sloshed hot chocolate over her last clean pair of jeans. Her feet had been propped up on a bale of hay and she'd been moaning to Nova (her favourite reindeer) about her list-loving brother, Nick.

Their mum and dad (Mrs and Mr Claus) were away from the North Pole on a sleigh-buying expedition. The old sleigh had broken down and even though Mum had fixed it temporarily (she was brilliant like that) Dad said that they had to get a new one immediately because of the schedule – Clara's family was obsessed with schedules. Anyway, Nick had been left in charge (because he was the oldest) and this morning Clara had been forced to listen to another lecture on 'putting things in the right places'. Apparently the floor wasn't the right place for dirty clothes.

'I'm over here!' she called out.

'Where's your radio?' demanded Nick as he came rushing around the corner behind Jingles.

Clara frowned. 'My what?'

'Your radio,' Nick snapped. 'You know, the one that you're supposed to have switched on and with you at all times, especially with Mum and Dad gone for the week. Clara, we've been

 8

trying to get hold of you for the past twenty-nine minutes!' Her brother waved a big black phone thingy in the air.

'Oh! You mean the Christmas-talkie!' Clara finally understood. 'It's right here, just as it should be.' She picked it up from the hay bale next to her and waggled it at her brother. Clara wondered what the cookies was going on. First Jingles burst in all flustered and now Nick was asking her questions about radios. This was supposed to be their quiet time of the year – there couldn't possibly be another crisis to deal with, not in March!

'Then why's it not working?' Nick grabbed the radio off her and flicked some buttons. 'Clara! It's dead.' He glared at his sister. 'You're supposed to charge it every night, remember?'

 9

'I did charge it!' Clara rose to her feet. 'But maybe I forgot to switch the plug on…' (She couldn't remember everything.)

Nick sighed. (*That was another job he'd have to do from now on, he thought to himself.*)

'Clara,' Jingles interrupted the bickering pair. 'We've got a problem. It's Rowan. I… I think she's in danger.'

Clara gasped. No wonder Jingles was so worried. Rowan was one of the kindest, sweetest (and chattiest) forest elves that Clara had ever met. Forest elves didn't live at the North Pole, they lived in forests, hence their name. But Rowan had been here to visit Jingles a few times because they were cousins and the only family each other had.

'What's happened?' she asked.

Jingles pressed a button on his radio and Rowan's voice filled the stables.

'Jingles, it's me. Listen, there's a bit of a problem and I—' A weird hissing sound echoed across the stables as Rowan's message crackled in and out of signal. Clara looked over at her brother, who put a finger to his lips. Rowan's voice blared out of the radio again. One word this time. *'Help.'*

Clara felt sick. 'We need to call her right away. Give me your radio thingy,' she demanded.

'We've already tried that,' said Nick. (*Honestly, did Clara think he was stupid or something?*) 'Rowan's not answering.'

'We have to do something, Clara,' said Jingles. 'I'm really worried.'

'Don't worry. I won't let anything happen to Rowan,' promised Clara. Her mind raced as she tried to think of a solution. 'We'll take the sleigh and—'

'Mum and Dad have the sleigh, remember?' Nick reminded her.

'Oh.' Clara felt her tummy sink and she nibbled her bottom lip. 'So… we'll just call them to come home—'

'We can't call them,' interrupted Nick again. 'They seem to care as much about their radios as *you* do, as they didn't take them, and they're not due back for another three days. We can't wait that long because… well, there's something else that you should know.'

Something else? thought Clara. *Just how bad can it get? We're already missing an elf!*

'Rowan left the message for me two days ago,' Jingles confessed.

'Two days!' Clara was beginning to panic.

'Like everyone else around here, Jingles didn't have his radio switched on,' Nick said pointedly.

'I honestly don't know why we bother to have these radios if no one is going to use them properly. I know they're new, but you'd think that after Christmas almost being cancelled last year—'

'Nick! You're not helping!' Clara hissed at her brother.

Jingles looked as if he was going to cry as he added, 'It gets worse too. Rowan is in charge of the Santa Scouts this year.'

Clara's mouth dropped open. 'Oh! That is worse.' She sank down back onto the hay.

Santa Scouts were fluffy little robin redbreasts who watched to see if children were being naughty or nice during the year, and reported back at Christmas time. Each year a particular forest elf was chosen to look after the Scouts, which meant training them, feeding them, keeping them warm and giving them buckets full of attention. Without the right training, the secret Scouts might be spotted and the lists could go wrong and if that happened… Christmas would be ruined! What were they going to do?

'I don't think I need to remind you how important the Scouts' schedule is, Clara,' Nick remarked.

'But it's just a few days,' Clara said.

'Every day counts!' Nick squeaked.

Jingles nodded. 'It takes a lot of practice to be a Scout – they must learn to listen and watch without anybody noticing. Plus the whole cute head-tilt thing they use to distract people.'

'Okay, so we need to find Rowan, make sure she's all right and check that the Scouts haven't missed any training.' Clara looked over at her brother. 'There's only one solution. I'm going to the forest.'

'I'll come with you,' Jingles announced, and he began to saddle up Nova, Clara's most trusted reindeer.

'Jingles.' Clara touched his arm gently. 'I need you here to make sure the rest of the reindeer are okay.'

'But you can't go alone,' the elf argued.

'She won't.' Nick looked determinedly at the pair.

Clara's eyes widened to the size of chocolate chip cookies. *Oh snowballs*, she thought. *Nick. On a reindeer. This is going to be interesting.*

Chapter Two

Hungry Seagulls

Clara and Nick galloped across the snow on Nova, Nick gripping tight to Clara's waist. There were no sides to hold on to on reindeer like there were on a sleigh.

'Up, Nova!' Clara ordered. Her stomach dropped as they lifted up high into the air.

'Clara, slow down!' Nick yelled in her ear as she swerved sharply to the right, narrowly avoiding some barnacle geese.

'I can't slow down, Nick! We're flying!'

The cold air whooshed through Clara's hair and she grinned. There was nothing like flying on a reindeer. She felt weightless as Nova tilted to the side. Nick grabbed on tighter and gave directions to Clara. He was in charge of navigation, being the map reader of the pair. She turned to look at him and had to swallow a giggle – Nick's eyes were clenched shut!

'Nick, how can you know where we're going if you can't see where we are?'

He gritted his teeth. 'Just go left, Clara!'

'Left, Nova,' she repeated, pulling on the reigns. A flock of seagulls swarmed around them. 'Up!' Clara shrieked. Nova pulled them up swiftly, but the seagulls simply soared higher and followed.

'Argh!' squealed Nick behind her.

Clara couldn't focus on her brother right now. The seagulls had begun cawing at them, clearly unwilling to share the sky with a reindeer and two children. Closer and closer they flew, circling Nova, Clara, and Nick.

'Down!' Clara ordered, trying to dodge away.

SQUAWK!

The seagulls flapped in mid-air, hovering over the trio before taking aim and dive-bombing down.

'Watch out, Clara! They're too close!'

 19

'I know that, Nick.' Clara held on tighter to Nova's reigns as she tried to outmanoeuvre the surging birds.

'Urgh!' Nick grimaced and ducked to the side. 'Clara, I nearly got pooped on – do something!'

'I am doing something!' she yelled back.

'Well, do something else! It's not working!'

Clara gritted her teeth and swooped to the right. The birds followed. She swooped left, then right again, weaving in and out of clouds. Still the birds came, honing in on them. One plucky gull headed straight towards Nova. Her reindeer whined as the bird began pecking at her.

'Right, that's it!' Clara reached across and rummaged in the satchel she'd brought, pulling out a chocolate spread sandwich that Nick had made for the journey. 'Break this up!' she called

over her shoulder, handing the sandwich to her brother. 'Throw it as far away from us as you can!'

'I spent ages making those sandwiches,' murmured Nick in her ear.

Nick threw the first piece of Clara's dinner. In a flash, the gulls pivoted and dived down after it, and Clara breathed out with relief. They squawked and flapped at each other, fighting over the food. Nick kept pelting bits of sandwich at them and the gulls had soon forgotten about the reindeer-riding children in their sky.

'Well done, Nick,' Clara panted. She reached forward to stroke Nova's neck. 'Are you okay?' she asked her reindeer and Nova nodded in response.

Nick checked his watch. 'Now we're going to be even later! By my calculations it will take

 21

another two hours to get to Rowan's house.'

Clara gulped and flew on. They had a job to do and she wasn't going to let Rowan or the Scouts down.

At last Clara and Nick landed with a thud in an empty forest. Tall trees stood proudly, their fresh green leaves illuminated by the sun glistening behind them.

'Good job, Nova,' Clara praised her reindeer, stroking her velvet-soft head. She checked to make sure Nova hadn't been hurt after their encounter with the seagulls. 'You can open your eyes now, Nick.' Clara grinned at her brother.

'My eyes were open Clara,' Nick retorted, 'mostly.'

Clara clamped her lips together to hide her smile as she swung her leg over Nova's back and jumped down onto the hard ground below. 'Are you sure this is the right place?' she asked, unwinding the red woollen scarf from her neck and looking around the forest.

'Of course we're in the right place,' her brother scoffed. (*Nick was particularly proud of his map-reading abilities. Finding a secret spot in the centre of a hidden forest in the middle of Dorset was not the easiest of tasks, thank you very much, but he'd done it. Even with his eyes closed.*)

Nick scoured the forest. 'It has to be around here somewhere!' He pursed his lips. They were looking for a house. Rowan's house to be precise.

A twig snapped behind them. Nick spun around and Clara gasped. They watched, their mouths hanging open, as a small brownish-grey creature with the bushiest tail Clara had ever seen leapt over from one high branch to the tree opposite.

'What was that?' exclaimed Clara. 'Did you see how it flew across like… like a mini flying reindeer? And then it just landed like it was no bother at all! What was it?'

'I think,' said Nick, flipping open his notebook, 'it was a squirrel.'

Clara crinkled her nose. 'Squirrel' was a cute name for such a fearless animal. Surely something like a 'fantastic flying fluff tail' would have been more appropriate. Clara watched in amazement as the creature leapt from branch to branch, before scurrying down a tree trunk head first, using its tail to balance. The squirrel halted, cupped its paws to its mouth, which Clara thought was the most adorable thing ever, then sprung off. *Cookies and cocoa!* Clara shook her head. The squirrel was like a tiny superhero.

'Squirrels are awesome!' she decided.

Clara turned and her eyes began to sparkle at the sight in front of her. Through the trees, the sun shone like a beacon. Rays of light spread across the forest floor, lighting up spots of yellow where daffodils bloomed. Clara walked forwards slowly, revelling at the sticks and twigs, rocks, and stones beneath her feet. No snow lay on the ground. No frost on the trees. The sky showed no sign of the thick, heavy snow clouds that she was so used to.

'Wow,' she gasped. Clara had never seen anything like it before. Nova nudged Clara's hand with her head and Clara stroked her reindeer absent-mindedly, unable to tear her gaze from the beauty before her.

Trees towered above, surrounding them with browns and greens. Drops of dew glistened in the sun, making the leaves sparkle and shine, and an unfamiliar floral scent filled the air. It was mesmerising. It was glorious. It was what Clara had read about in books ever since she was little and had always wanted to see. It was Spring.

'Come on,' Nick said, interrupting Clara's wonder. He turned to his left, following a narrow path below branches that had grown into an arch over the top of them, as if holding hands.

'Um, where are you going?' asked Clara, walking behind her brother.

'It's this way,' he replied, pushing aside an overgrown bramble that had begun to cover a path to the right.

'Are you sure?' Clara crinkled her nose. She had spotted something. Hidden amongst the trees was a cottage. Clara narrowed her eyes, trying to get a better look. Nick followed her gaze and his whole face changed as delight washed over it.

'I found it!' he announced loudly.

Clara bit her tongue. Technically, *she* had found it. But she decided, rather kindly, not to correct her brother.

As they walked closer towards the cottage, Clara could see the walls were painted pale yellow with black beams running across them in a diagonal pattern that met in the middle. The house was partially covered by a willow tree and a small stream trickled beside it.

It was no gingerbread house like her house in the North Pole, but it still had the familiar warmth of someone's beloved home.

'Rowan?' Nick called out, knocking on the green front door.

Only silence greeted him. A shiver ran up Clara's neck. 'Didn't Jingles say there was an aviary at the side of the house for the Scouts?' she asked. 'I can't hear any birds, Nick!'

'I'll go and check.' Nick nodded. 'You stay here and feed Nova.'

Clara smiled at her brother, grateful he remembered her reindeer.

She got Nova settled and fed her a carrot from her satchel whilst looking at her surroundings. Despite the worry, Clara couldn't help but smile. It was all so green and colourful! It even smelt different. And despite there being lots of strange and interesting new scents in the air, Clara was sure she could smell something incredibly familiar… the sweet and extremely delicious aroma of chocolate. *How very odd*, she thought to herself.

CHAPTER THREE

A Clue!

'There's no sign of Rowan or the Scouts anywhere,' Nick announced as he came back. 'The aviary is empty.' He was holding his notebook in his hand and Clara guessed just what was coming next. 'I've written a list.'

Clara nibbled her lip. She knew it! Only Nick could turn every problem into an opportunity to make a list. 'Let's see it then,' she sighed.

Nick held his notebook open for Clara.

Nick Claus Junior's list of how to find the Scouts and Rowan the forest elf

Job one: Look for clues

'We've not had a proper look around the house yet,' Nick explained, 'and we might find something to help us figure out what happened.'

Clara nodded in agreement and looked back down at the notebook.

Job Two: Search the forest

'I realise it's a big forest,' Nick said. 'So we should probably search together so you don't get lost.'

Clara gaped at her brother. As if she would ever get lost!

Nick flipped shut his notebook and put it back in his pocket.

Is that it? Clara thought, pursing her lips. *Look for clues and search the forest?* Surely they

 32

didn't need a list to tell them that. But Clara shrugged and smiled at her brother. She knew making lists was Nick's way of getting rid of all the worry from inside his brain – Mum had told her that after the whole Christmas-list fiasco a few months ago.

'Okay, let's search the house,' she said as brightly as she could.

The first thing that Clara noticed when she opened the door was that the smell of chocolate was stronger inside. Her stomach growled and she thought of the sandwich she'd sacrificed to escape the seagulls.

Rowan's house was simple. In the lounge there was a small sofa scattered with cushions alongside a bookcase heaving with books, and in the kitchen stood a wooden table and two chairs.

As Clara looked for signs of Rowan, she noticed that there were flowers dotted around the kitchen in small pots. *How pretty!* she thought as she walked over and took a deep breath.

'The white ones are snowdrops,' explained Nick. 'The blue ones are bluebells and the yellow ones are daffodils.'

'They look like golden fairy lights.' Clara grinned as she bent to take a closer look. That was when she spotted little pieces of something wrapped in pink that were stacked up on the side. They had the initials 'E.B.' stamped on the front in swirly writing. Clara practically drooled from the incredible smell coming from them: chocolate. Her stomach growled again and Clara couldn't help herself.

Checking to see if Nick was looking (phew, he wasn't), Clara took a piece of the chocolate, quietly unwrapping it and popping it into her mouth.

Oh. My. Cookies. The chocolate melted on her tongue and coated every single taste bud in delicious creamy scrumminess. This had to be the most mouth-watering chocolate that Clara had ever eaten. And she'd eaten a lot.

'I'll check the garden,' Nick called over to her. Clara nodded, her mouth full of chocolate. 'Are you all right?' her brother asked, peering closely at her.

'Mmm-hmm.' Clara tried to grin without showing her chocolate-covered teeth and made a show of opening drawers for clues. As soon as she was sure that Nick was outside, Clara grabbed another chocolate and popped it in her mouth. Her taste buds danced with glee.

'Clara!' her brother yelled, interrupting Clara's chocolate-chomping feast.

'I've found a clue!'

She raced outside and Nick held out his hand, revealing another wrapped chocolate, bright green this time. 'It says "E.B." on the front. What do you think that means?' he asked.

'Why don't we eat it and see?' Clara replied eagerly.

'Eat it?' Nick's eyes narrowed. 'How do you know it's food?'

'It's chocolate,' Clara confessed. 'I found some in the kitchen too.'

'Clara! Have you been eating the clues?!'

'Only some of them,' she admitted. 'But you have to try it, Nick – it's amazing.'

'I will do no such thing. We've got a job to do!' (*Honestly, he thought, now wasn't the time to stop for snacks.*) 'Show me where you found the other pieces.'

Clara led the way back to the front door, but stopped when she noticed something stuck in the hedgerow by the path. It was a note, written on green paper. She attempted to prise it free but realised it was soaking wet.

'It must have rained last night,' Nick said.

 37

'What does it say?'

Clara tried to make out some of the words, but it was tricky – the ink had run and splurged together in places. The only words she could read were 'help', 'taken', 'E.B.', and 'help' again.

Clara gasped as fear washed over her. 'Rowan and the Scouts have been taken by this E.B. character!'

Nick snatched the note and read it for himself. 'I think you're right!'

'The poor robins will be terrified,' Clara said. 'Oh, Nick, what are we going to do?' Clara shivered despite the warmth. This adventure was turning out to be even more worrisome than she'd thought.

CHAPTER FOUR

Trapped

Clara and Nick ran out into the forest, hoping to catch a glimpse of something – anything that would help them find Rowan and the Scouts. Clara had brought Nova with them – there was no way she would leave her reindeer alone when there was danger about.

'Whoa!' Nick cried as he skidded backwards in a puddle. His legs flailed in the air as his arms flapped like a broken propeller. He landed on the ground with a splodgy thud, mud splattering everywhere. 'Argh!' he groaned.

Clara burrowed her face into Nova's neck, hiding her laughter at the sight of her brother covered head to toe in brown sludgy mud. He looked like some sort of chocolate snowman. *A mudman!* Clara chortled to herself. 'Oh, Nick,' she snorted and hid her face again. 'Are you okay?'

'No, I am not okay. I'm filthy, Clara. I'm cold and wet and really, really... icky!' He scrambled to his feet, sliding so much on the slippery mud that Clara was sure he was going to tumble again.

'Go inside and put some of Rowan's clothes on,' she ordered, turning her brother around and pushing him back towards the house. She knew they'd never get anything done until her brother was neat and tidy again. 'Go on!' she repeated. Nick trudged away, dripping mud as he went.

Left on her own, Clara studied their surroundings. It was getting dark already, and now she found the forest less appealing. The air had a tinge of winter about it, which should have brought comfort to her, but strangely it did not. There was nothing jolly about the forest at dusk, thought Clara. Now the branches seemed to be reaching out towards *her* rather than holding hands. The flowers had closed up, removing the colour and with it the joy. There were no familiar sounds of reindeer or chortling elves to soothe her – just squawks and caws of unfamiliar birds.

Nick broke her unease by striding out of the house in the most extraordinary outfit Clara had ever seen. Rowan must have been much shorter than she remembered because Nick was wearing trousers that finished just below his knees and a bright green top that stopped

 41

above his belly button, no matter how much Nick kept tugging it down.

'Don't say a word.' Nick glared at her, brushing past and switching on his torch.

Clara could've kissed Nick for remembering to bring a torch but obviously didn't because – yuk! Instead she huddled up a little closer to her brother as they continued to search for the elusive E.B.

On they walked, ducking under branches and trampling past prickly bushes that kept catching on their clothes and yanking them back. Poor Nova was plodding slowly behind, unable to avoid the whacks of the thorny plants either.

Finally they came to a clearing. Clara turned, and was about to tell Nova that there were no more brambles for now when the ground suddenly vanished beneath her.

'Oompf!' Clara and Nick both yelped as they went flying up into the air. *What's happening!* she thought. Clara thrashed around, realising they were scooped up together, tumbled inside a net which was swinging high in a tree.

They'd been caught in a trap!

'E.B.'s captured us!' yelled Clara as she flailed and flapped around like a fish. They both kicked, shoved, and pushed, trying to free themselves. Clara heard a panicked reindeer grunt from below.

'Nova!' she shrieked, terrified for her reindeer. What if E.B. tried to trap Nova too? She peered through a gap in the netting and saw Nova was safe on the ground – albeit a little twitchy at the sight of her two humans stuck up high in a tree. Clara wriggled and she squirmed, desperate to get down to comfort her reindeer, which only resulted in Clara and Nick banging into each other more. Now they were swinging from side to side even harder. 'Ow!' Clara cried as her brown hair got tangled behind Nick's elbow.

'Stop it, Clara!' hollered Nick. 'You're making it worse.'

'Oh, I'm sorry, Nick. I didn't realise there was a proper way to escape a net. Please do show me,' she snapped.

'Look. You've just got to…' Nick managed to wiggle his arm free from beneath him, although he did have to stick his tongue out and waggle it relentlessly in the air to do so. Eurgh, thought Clara. 'Now I'm going to…' He reached out his free arm and pushed his fingers through a hole in the net.

'How's it going, Nick?' Clara asked, her eyebrows raised.

'That's not helpful,' he panted. 'Urgh! Nothing works!'

'Well, something better work soon, Nick!

Nova is terrified down there and I'm not letting E.B. get a hold of her.' Clara nibbled her bottom lip. 'How are we going to find the missing birds now? And poor Rowan is out there somewhere too, cold and afraid!'

'You've no idea where Rowan is,' Nick pointed out. 'She could be somewhere warm and cosy.' Clara stared at her brother. 'Well, she could be!'

'Oh, I'll radio Jingles right now, shall I, and tell him that we don't know where his cousin or the Scouts are, but it's all right because Nick thinks they might all be warm!'

'Stop shrieking!' Nick jerked in the net, trying to free himself, but instead more leaves stuck to his face.

'I am not shrieking!' Clara shrieked.

Thud! Thud! Thud!

 46

Clara and Nick froze and slowly looked towards the direction of the noise.

Thud! Thud! Thud!

'Nick…' Clara's voice shook as she stared into the distance. 'What's that?'

Trees juddered around them as Clara's heart pounded like the shuddering ground below. Through the bushes burst one of the scariest creatures Clara had ever seen. It looked kind of human but with a red and blotchy face. Its eyes bulged wide. Drool dribbled down the side of its mouth. And most terrifying of all was this thing was heading straight towards Nova.

CHAPTER FIVE

The Gnome

The creature stopped as soon as it saw Nova. Clara's heart froze in fear at the sight of her beautiful reindeer alone with this petrifying beast. Was this E.B.?

'Hello there, pretty,' it said to the reindeer, its voice soft and gentle and not at all what Clara expected.

Clara watched her reindeer nestle into the creature's hand and warmth flooded back through her as she realised that Nova wasn't in any danger.

'What have you done with the robins?' the creature bellowed up at the tree whilst still stroking Nova.

'What have *you* done with them, more like?' Clara yelled back.

'Me?' the creature growled. It stormed out of sight and then...

Whoosh!

Clara felt herself falling (which wasn't as much fun as flying).

'Argh!' she cried.

'Argh!' Nick screamed.

Whoopf! Thud!

It was over. The creature had released them and Clara and Nick found themselves safely on the ground (if a little bruised).

'Ow!' howled Clara. Nick rubbed his cheek where his sister's elbow had thrust into it, accidentally of course, whilst Clara relished the reindeer licks she was getting all over her leaf-covered face. 'Why the daffodils did you trap us in a net, E.B.?'

Clara saw now that the creature wasn't actually as terrifying as she'd first thought. In front of them stood a man with a white beard. His hair, also white, was curly and cut short. He was stocky in build and wearing brown dungarees, a khaki and yellow checked shirt and heavy black boots.

'E who? And why do you think I caught you?' the man sneered.

Clara scowled. She knew exactly why – to stop them from discovering the truth: that he was a thief who stole robins and elves. Clara was about to give him a piece of her mind when Nick piped up.

'Um, forgive me for asking,' he said as he clambered back onto his feet. 'But aren't you a gnome?'

'What's it to do with you?' The gnome folded his arms.

'I knew it!' Nick punched the air. 'I've never met a gnome before. How thrilling. Clara, can you believe it? A real-life gnome! Hello, I'm Nick.' He went to shake the gnome's hand but was met with a glare instead.

Clara stared at her brother. 'Nick, I don't care who he is, he's stolen the Scouts!'

'But that's just it, Clara, he can't have stolen the Scouts. Gnomes look after animals, they don't hurt them! Well, except for cats of course.' Nick snickered. *He actually snickered. What the cookies was wrong with him?* thought Clara. *There was nothing funny about their current predicament, thank you very much.* 'We're perfectly safe with a gnome,' her brother added.

'All right then.' Clara placed her hands on her hips. 'What's a gnome?'

Nick looked at her as if she had sprouted reindeer antlers. 'A gnome. You know, as in *gnomes*.'

Nick could say 'gnome' as much as he liked, thought Clara, she still didn't know what he was going on about. At this point, Nick began to babble on and on (and on) about gnomes, but to save you having to listen to all that (you're

 52

welcome), here are the highlights…

Interesting facts about gnomes,
chosen by Clara Claus (as told by Nick)

FACT ONE: Gnomes love animals – in fact they consider themselves animal protectors. Which is kind of lovely actually.

FACT TWO: They rescue animals in distress. If you know of any animal in trouble, you're best to tell a gnome.

FACT THREE: Gnomes can talk to most animals. How amazing would it be to have a conversation with an animal? (Clara thought of all the chats she could have with Nova!)

FACT FOUR: Gnomes don't like cats in any way. Weird, huh?

FACT FIVE: They're grumpy. Pretty obvious after Clara and Nick's first encounter with one.

FACT SIX: Gnomes like maps. (Not that interesting a fact, but Nick really wanted it on the list as he liked maps too and it was always nice to find shared interests.)

 53

'So you see, a gnome would never steal the Scouts,' Nick said after his babbling.

'That's right, I wouldn't,' grumbled the gnome. 'And my name's Gordon, not Gnome.'

'Okay,' said Clara slowly, distracted by Nick's face, which had gone completely white as he gasped loudly. 'Nick,' she hissed. 'What are you doing? Why are you holding your bottom?'

'I'm n-not holding my b-bottom,' he stammered. 'I'm covering it.'

Clara didn't understand, but Gordon did.

'You've ripped your pants!' he hollered so loudly that it echoed through the trees. (*So loudly, Nick was sure that the elves could hear it in the North Pole.*)

Oh, poor Nick, thought Clara, trying not to giggle as she handed her red scarf to her brother. Nick gratefully wrapped it around himself like a skirt.

'Come on.' Gordon gestured to the children and took Nova by the reigns. 'You can borrow something of mine. I don't know why you're wearing such small clothes anyway!' he muttered. 'Then you can tell me what you've done with those birds.'

Clara frowned as they set off. If Gordon didn't have the Scouts, and Clara and Nick didn't have the Scouts, then who did?

Chapter Six

House in a Tree

Clara didn't get a chance to ask her question. She was too busy concentrating on the path now it was too dark to see. The sun had gone completely, and all they had was the light from Nick's torch.

'Ow,' Clara cried, tripping on a root protruding from the ground. She was feeling more and more out of sorts by the second. Clara was used to fairy lights twinkling and lamps shining, snow falling and elves singing. Everything was different here. In the daylight it had been beautiful: colourful flowers and green all around. In the darkness, she could feel the forest closing in on her. She didn't mind admitting that it was a little scary. Clara couldn't believe it was only that morning she'd been playing in the stables with the reindeer. And though Clara liked adventure, she had never spent a night away from the North Pole and she was feeling a little squirmy inside. She missed home. But she had to continue. What would happen to Rowan and the robins if she didn't? She imagined how scared poor Rowan must be feeling.

Gordon had been walking ahead with her brother whilst Nick explained who they were and why they were here, but now he stopped at the base of an enormous oak tree. Clara could just about make out a strange bright orange marking on the bark. He knocked three times, then did a sort of odd whistle though his teeth,

 57

followed by a *rat-a-tat-tat*. A door opened from the base of the tree and Gordon ducked inside. Clara perked up. Had a tree just opened up in front of them like magic? *Wowzee wow-wow. A house in a tree! You don't get that at the North Pole!* Her fears disappeared, pushed down by feelings of excitement and wonder. Clara looked over at her brother's open mouth and smiled slightly. She wasn't the only one who was amazed. Even Nova couldn't stop staring.

When she stepped inside, Clara's mouth dropped open.

Gordon's house was enormous – especially considering it was inside a tree. Gordon took Nova's reigns and led her off to the indoor stables. Clara made a note in her head to mention it to Mum when they got back home. Indoor stables! It was at times like this that she wished she had a notebook like Nick, to write things down so she wouldn't forget them.

Flickering lamps hung in strings around the treehouse, giving a comforting glow. Clara could feel her insides settle as she looked around. There were books everywhere: in piles, on shelves and even on a train that appeared to run around the outside of the living room. The train looked big enough to sit on. (Clara decided it was the coolest thing ever.)

Gordon saw Clara looking. 'Go on,' he

 59

chuckled. 'You can go on it if you like. That little red button is the brake when you want to stop.'

Not needing to be told twice, Clara swung her legs over the train carriage, sitting on a black cushioned seat.

As the little train chugged around, Clara got to see more of Gordon's home. On the other side of a tunnel lay a bridge across a stream. Above that was a waterfall. Water bounced into a small pond of water lilies, causing them to bob like birds on the ocean. Flowers and vines adorned the bridge.

'Choo! Choo!' Clara called and waved as she whizzed past Nova.

Nova nodded but was far too busy chomping on moss in the straw-laden stables to look up. Three times Clara whooshed round the house on the train before reaching out and pressing the red button. The train slowed and then let out a delightful four-note tune, which it repeated four times, each time getting slower until finally screeching to a stop.

Clara jumped off, buzzing from her ride and taking a drink that Nick handed to her. She noticed that her brother had now changed into some of Gordon's clothes – they were far too big for him, but at least he was clean and his bottom was covered.

He was giving Clara a weird look: his eyes kept widening and narrowing a bit like a nutcracker and he was kind of shaking his head at her but at the same time barely moving. Clara shrugged – she was too hungry and thirsty to try to work this out.

Smiling at her brother and raising her glass at Gordon, Clara took a sip of the drink and immediately wished she hadn't. What the seagull feathers was that?

Gordon smiled. 'Lovely, isn't it? It's my special brew.'

Clara managed to gulp the disgusting liquid down. 'Oh, wow.' She cleared her throat, trying to get the taste out of her mouth and wishing that she'd worked out Nick's silent warning. 'It's um… unusual. We don't have anything like this where we come from.' Clara was used to hot chocolate, candy canes, and cookies. This tasted a bit like one of those special teas that Mum made Dad drink when he had trouble sleeping. Clara didn't say any of that though. Instead she said, 'It's lovely. What, er, is it?'

Gordon puffed out his chest like a robin would. 'It's made of apple blossoms, crunched into mulch. Hard to come by these days. With bee spit and morning dew.'

'Bee spit?' Clara spluttered.

'Oh yes – before it's made into honey. Much nicer, isn't it? And a lot less sweet.'

Clara glared at Nick. (*He was biting the inside of his cheek as hard as he could to stop himself snorting. It didn't work.*)

He turned his body away but Clara could see his shoulders shaking up and down. She wanted to kick him, but instead Clara turned to Gordon. They needed to talk about Rowan and the Scouts. Now she knew Gordon was a gnome, she was certain they could trust him, especially after his kindness to Nova and his hospitality to them. But before she could begin, the strangest thing happened. Gordon started talking to a rock!

CHAPTER SEVEN

Rocky

'It's all right, Rocky, my lass.' Gordon held open his top breast pocket and spoke into it.

Clara and Nick stared at each other.

'Um, are you okay, Mr Gordon sir?' asked Nick, edging away a little. (*Nothing that he'd read suggested gnomes talked to rocks. He wondered if they spoke to plants too or maybe it was just a mineral thing...*)

'The name's plain Gordon and yes, I'm perfectly fine. Rocky here is just a little spooked, aren't you, little lady?' He caressed his pocket. 'Would you like to meet her?'

Clara didn't know what to say. (She'd never

met a pet rock before.)

Thankfully Nick took charge. 'Hello, Rocky.' Nick waved at Gordon's pocket. 'Lovely to meet you!'

'Who's he talking to?' Gordon looked at Clara.

'Um, Rocky,' she replied.

'Well, wait until I've got her out,' he bristled. 'My, you two are very strange.'

We're very strange? thought Clara. *You're the one with the pet rock!* She didn't say that though – she simply smiled and waited politely whilst Gordon delved into his top pocket and got out… a teeny tiny robin.

'I've had Rocky here ever since she was a fledgling. She can't fly, you see,' Gordon whispered. 'She has a damaged wing.'

'But she's a bird!' Nick said. (*All robins flew,*

didn't they, he thought?) Clara nudged Nick for being so rude.

'Now listen here, you,' Gordon said. 'Rocky is a very clever bird – aren't you, my fluffy little Rocky-kins?' Gordon was talking in a strange way that Clara had only ever heard before from her mum, when Mrs Claus had been holding a baby elf. Rocky seemed to love every second and was rubbing her head into Gordon's hand. 'She just can't fly, can you my little rock star? That's all.'

'A bit weird though, isn't it?' said Nick. Clara elbowed him harder this time. But she didn't need to worry – Rocky wasn't going to let him get away with it.

The little robin hopped over to the bottom of Nick's feet and chirped furiously. All Nick could do was gape at Rocky, which was obviously not good enough for the plucky bird. Before he knew it, the robin began to peck at Nick's toes. Clara was relieved that Nick was wearing shoes, but then Rocky, being a bright bird, began pecking at Nick's ankles instead.

'Ow!' he howled. 'Stop it.'

'Tweet, tweet, tweet! Tweet, tweet, tweet, tweet!'

'That's right, you tell him,' cheered Gordon.

The sweet creature began pulling at Nick's (actually Gordon's) trousers, which were far too loose and very easily pulled down, especially by a rather cross robin.

'Stop!' Nick hollered as he tried to keep his trousers up with his hands. 'Please stop. I'm sorry!'

Clara couldn't help herself. She tried, oh feathers did she try, but her brother getting a proper telling off from the cutest, smallest, fluffiest creature ever was just too funny not to laugh at. She hooted and guffawed, she snorted and hollered. Her stomach ached with joy. Soon they were all laughing except for poor Nick. Luckily, Rocky's peck was not as bad as it looked and all Nick suffered was a few scratches. Having made her point, Rocky stopped pecking and hopped over to Gordon, who scooped her up and placed her on his shoulder.

Clara took her chance

to speak, the grin falling from her face – they had to find out what had happened to their friend.

'Do you know Rowan and the Scouts?' she asked Gordon – and Rocky, in case she could understand her.

'Of course I do – they live not far from here. Rowan's…well, she's a bit too chatty for my liking, but she's brilliant with Rocky. We haven't seen the Scouts for a few days, which is why I set a trap. Sorry again about that by the way.' Gordon winced. Clara waved her hand, brushing the apology away. The gnome suddenly bolted upright. 'Wait, who's E.B.?' he asked. 'I remember you saying you thought I was E.B. Who is that?'

Nick explained all about the note they'd found from the mysterious E.B.

Gordon began pacing, Rocky chirruping in his ear. With the bird on his shoulder, Clara thought the gnome looked like some sort of strange pirate.

'Do you still have the note?' Gordon asked, stroking his beard.

'Of course.' Nick flipped open his notebook. 'I kept it just in case.' He smiled smugly at his sister.

Clara grinned. 'Well, you were bound to have a good idea sooner or later!'

Nick glared at his sister. 'Clara,' he warned.

'Yes, Nick,' she answered sweetly.

'Stick a cookie in it.'

Clara smiled at Nick then wished she did have a cookie. She was ravenous!

'I've got just the thing to help us.' Gordon

 73

winked at Nick and tapped his nose. He took the wax part of a candle and a handful of red berries then ground them together into a mulch. Next, he added some water, mixed the solution again and finally brushed the strange concoction all over the note. The green paper turned a deep shade of red, all except for where the words had been written, which were now all green and completely visible!

'That's amazing!' Nick stared at the paper for a moment before writing notes in his book frantically. (*He was fascinated by the science of it all.*)

'Nick! The letter!' Clara reminded him.

He hastily put his notebook away and crowded by Clara as they both read:

Dear Clara,

Thank you so much for coming. As I explained in my message to Jingles, the Easter Bunny needs our help urgently. It's his first year delivering all the eggs, but he was only made Easter Bunny three weeks ago, and he doesn't know what to do! Fancy the old Easter Bunny retiring so close to Easter, eh?

I was hoping to wait for you to arrive, but it's taken you longer than I expected and we cannot waste any more time. Easter is just five days away and E.B. needs our help immediately! The happiness of children depends on it!

Meet us in the meadow on the hill. Please hurry.

Rowan

'So E.B. is the Easter Bunny!' realised Clara. 'That's why the chocolate was so tasty.'

'Well, it all makes sense now.' Gordon nodded to himself. 'I was wondering who would be taking over from Bill.'

What makes sense? wondered Clara. *And who the daffodils is Bill?*

'Um, who?' asked Nick, a little more politely than Clara would have done.

'Bill was the old Easter Bunny,' Gordon explained. 'Last month he just upped and left. Found a chocolate factory and wanted to run it with all of his bunnies. So that's what he did.' Gordon shrugged. 'I never really thought about the new Easter Bunny. The poor thing won't have a clue what to do!'

Nick frowned. 'So Rowan's not in danger at

all, she just needs our help.' He shook his head. 'Hmm, it's a little irresponsible to be taking the Scouts away from their training.'

'Nick!' Clara couldn't believe her brother sometimes. The new Easter Bunny needed help and that was what they were going to do. She knew how important Easter was to all the children around the world – almost as important as Christmas! And if helping meant eating more scrumptious chocolate, then Clara was more than happy to oblige.

'Do you know where the meadow on the hill is?' Nick asked Gordon.

The gnome nodded. 'But we can't go now – everyone knows that bunnies are early risers and go to bed as soon as darkness falls! We'll leave first thing in the morning.'

 77

With a plan in place, they all settled down for the night. Clara and Nick lay on the sofas in the lounge and snuggled into the blankets that Gordon had given them. Soon the room was filled with the sound of Nick snoring. That, together with the happiness of children at stake, meant Clara wasn't sure she'd be able to sleep a wink...

Chapter Eight

Bob

Surprisingly, Clara had slept well. Maybe it was something to do with being surrounded by nature – inside a tree no less! However, when she spoke to Jingles first thing on the radio to let him know that Rowan was safe and that they were going to save Easter, her calmness disappeared.

'But, Clara,' Jingles's voice crackled over the radio, 'Easter isn't five days away any more. It's two.'

'Two days!' Clara nibbled her lip. 'We'd better hop to it!'

The sun was glistening through the trees

 79

as they set off after a quick, not-so-great breakfast, due to Gordon's obsession with berries and bee spit. At least Nova was happy, thanks to Gordon's bountiful supply of moss.

Clara gazed around as they walked and took in deep breaths of the morning air – fresh but not icy freeze-you-to-the-toes fresh that Clara was used to. She was still fascinated by all the smells of flowers and plants and began reaching out her hand to touch a shiny tree that was almost silver. Hastily she snatched her hand back at the last moment. 'Does every tree have a gnome living in it?' she wondered.

'Of course not,' Gordon grumbled. 'Gnomes only live in oak trees – and that is clearly a silver birch. Besides, there aren't enough gnomes to fill every oak tree. Usually gnome trees have colours on them – markings like yellow, white, green or orange like mine.'

Nick opened his mouth (*he wanted to ask more questions*) but Gordon shushed him with a finger to his lips. 'Over there,' he whispered, pointing to a field.

'Why are we whispering?' Clara asked in hushed tones.

'We don't want to scare the rabbits,' Gordon replied.

Clara gasped as she peered through the leaves and saw a meadow bursting with daisies and buttercups. But that wasn't all – scattered amongst the flowers and tall grasses were hundreds of bunnies. Brown bunnies, black bunnies, white bunnies, grey bunnies.

 81

Clara even saw pink bunnies, which had Nick scratching his head. (*He was certain there was no such breed.*) Clara smiled to herself – her brother's need for explanation and scientific proof of everything was strange when they lived at the North Pole with Santa and magical flying reindeer.

Gordon began tutting rapidly with his tongue behind his front teeth which, to Clara, sounded suspiciously like a reindeer chomping down on a carrot. Soon she realised just what Gordon was doing: talking to the rabbits!

It clearly worked because hopping towards them, twitching its whiskers, was the cutest, fluffiest little brown bunny Clara had ever seen.

'Hello,' she sung softly, 'aren't you the

sweetest. My name's Clara – Clara Claus. What's yours, eh?' The bunny's ears pricked up so Clara crept closer. 'Is it Fluffikins? Because that's what you are – so very cute and fluffy.'

'Actually, it's Bob.' The voice was deep and loud and appeared to come from the rabbit. 'But, Clara Claus,' the rabbit continued, 'you might know me as E.B.'

One minute the bunny was small, the next minute it was big. Really big! Gigantic. Huge. *Daffodils and dandelions!* gulped Clara as she fell backwards onto the ground. What was going on? The bunny had magically changed before her eyes. It was at least one and a half times taller than Clara now, which for a bunny was pretty big.

 83

The rabbit bowed. 'It is an honour to meet the daughter of the great Santa Claus. The Easter Bunny at your service.'

Clara gawked at the giant bunny standing in front of her on his hind legs, his paws on his hips.

'Bob, hi.' Nick held out his hand. What was with all the hand shaking, wondered Clara. Nick seemed obsessed with it! 'I'm Santa's son. I've heard so much about you,' Nick went on. 'Well, I've made notes – would you like to see?'

Clara snorted in disbelief, accidentally sending some snot flying – but she couldn't believe it! How in icicles had Nick made notes so quickly? She'd seen him writing as Bob had been speaking, but there'd not been that much time. Clara glanced down at the notebook and saw that it was flipped to a page titled: 'Easter Bunny Facts'. Honestly, did Nick have a list for everything?!

Easter Bunny facts by Nick Claus Junior

Fact one: The Easter Bunny, or E.B. for short, is called Bob!

Bob!?! Clara thought. Not Whiskerkins or Cutiefluffypie, but Bob.

Fact Two: The Easter Bunny can shrink or grow to his actual height of five foot ten inches, which is 177.8 centimetres, the same height as Santa.

Clara wished she could shrink and grow whenever she liked. She'd be able to reach the cookies Mum always hid.

Fact Three: According to the Magical People Encyclopaedia, the Easter Bunny is scared of cats.

What was with all the cat-hating, wondered Clara?

Fact Four: E.B. only wears clothes in his giant form.

It took Clara a little while to notice this, but yes, the big, giant Easter Bunny was wearing a purple jumper, blue shirt, and pink bow tie.

Fact Five: Big basket fan.

That seemed obvious, thought Clara – where else was he going to put his eggs?

 87

Clara thought that being a giant bunny that could talk was pretty fantastic.

Clara had to admit that Easter was pretty great – it was no Christmas, but Clara thought it'd be lovely to hunt for eggs.

They didn't have egg hunts at the North Pole in case the reindeer found them – chocolate wasn't good for their tummies. The Claus family always

 88

made sure they had a special supper at Easter: melted chocolate with chopped up chunks of fresh fruit dunked in (Clara's absolute favourite was pineapple and chocolate – delicious!). Fruit was hard to come by at the North Pole so Dad always flew to Greenland to get some for an Easter treat. Clara was definitely going to suggest indoor egg hunts to her parents when they got back. She was just about to tell Nick her egg-cellent – ha! – plan… when Bob burst into big bunny tears.

CHAPTER NINE

Rabbit Tears

'Waaaaaa!' Bob wailed. Birds shot out from the trees and disappeared up into the sky.

Clara scowled at her brother. 'Nick, what did you say?' She'd stopped listening whilst she was reading Nick's list.

'I didn't say anything!' he protested. 'Just that we were from the North Pole, looking for Rowan, and that she'd left a message asking for us to help.'

'I do need help!' sobbed the bunny. 'I'm rubbish! I can't do it. I've tried, I really have, but...' He sobbed louder. 'I don't deserve to be the Easter Bunny and now no one's going to get any chocolate. No one! Easter will be ruined.'

No one's going to get any chocolate? Clara felt sick. That would be awful. Terrible! A disaster! She thought about how sad all the children would be...

'I don't even know what I'm supposed to do,' Bob continued. 'I've not had any training, you see. There weren't even any instructions! I only got the letter a few weeks ago telling me I'd been chosen as the new Easter Bunny. I just wanted to make chocolate for everyone. That's what I'm good at. Making chocolate. I love it and it makes people happy. I like making people happy.' His bottom lip began to quiver.

'Being an Easter Bunny was my dream job, but I never expected to become one so soon.

It's unheard of for an Easter Bunny to just leave with all their bunny helpers right before Easter and without even showing any other bunny what to do!' Bob plonked himself on the ground. 'It's all right for you with your magic and elves and reindeer and lists and stuff.'

Bob dabbed his eyes with the bottom of his waistcoat. 'You have an enormous team. I don't have any of that! I had to gather together all the bunnies I knew who were willing to help at the last minute! They've been painting and basket weaving and map drawing, but they've never done it before…'

'Maps?' Nick said. 'I like maps.' Clara glared at him.

'Do you know how many egg hunts there are?' Bob asked Clara and Nick. 'Hundreds!

Thousands! And they're not just outside, you know. They're in houses now too, and apartments – and parks, museums, beaches, schools, forests, shops... everywhere! And I'm just supposed to know what to do!'

'Is that why Rowan's here?' asked Clara gently. 'To help you?'

'She was walking in the woods and found me trying to make bunting. I'm not very good at that either. She told me all about you and how you saved Christmas and that you'd definitely help me. You will, won't you? Because I won't be able to do it otherwise.' He shook his head and looked up at Clara, his big brown bunny eyes brimming with tears.

'Of course we'll help you!' Clara put her arm around the sobbing rabbit. Poor Bob, having to learn everything from scratch.

'Where is Rowan by the way?' Nick butted in. 'And the Scouts? It's just that there is actually a schedule and they're quite behind now so—'

'Now's not the time, Nick!' Clara hissed.

Bob waved his hand in the air. 'Oh, they're somewhere around, trying to practise flying with the eggs,' he explained. 'But they're too heavy for the Scouts to carry!' Fresh sobs erupted from Bob, but Clara knew just what she was going to do.

'Bob,' she declared. 'I've got a plan. I—'

'Clara!' called out Rowan who was walking towards them, interrupting Clara's plan.

Clara raced towards the elf – she couldn't help herself. She was so relieved and excited to see Rowan. Her brother ran alongside her muttering something about training and schedules.

Rowan beamed. 'Oh, I'm so pleased to see you!' Scouts flew happily around her, tweeting and singing. Clara was thrilled to see that each and every one of them looked happy.

'I knew you'd come,' Rowan said with a grin. 'Although you are cutting it close, Easter being only two days away... Still, I'm sure you can work your magic, you know – do your thing and fix it. So are you? Going to fix it, I mean? Of course you are, what am I saying? It's just that I was wondering how because...'

Rowan's voice dropped to a whisper. 'The Scouts aren't really the best birds for the job. The chocolate eggs are a bit too heavy for them and I'm afraid Bob doesn't seem to be taking the challenges of his new job very well. He keeps crying and eating chocolate – and when I say *eating*, I mean *scoffing*, which isn't brilliant because obviously we need that chocolate for Easter. Then the rabbits have extra work to do – making, decorating and wrapping additional chocolate, so they're even more tired and—'

'Rowan!' interrupted Nick. Clara was grateful. She'd thought Rowan would never stop talking. 'You do know that the Scouts have missed three weeks' training? I cannot emphasise how important schedules are, even this far away from Christmas, and—'

'It's four weeks they've missed actually,' confessed Rowan. 'But don't worry, I've been doing some training here so we're not too far behind. And you can't put a schedule on helping people, can you, Nick? And you brought Nova! That's a brilliant idea, Clara. She could fly up to all the high places. How do you come up with such fantastic plans? They're marvellous! Excellent! That's what I told Bob. "*Clara will save the day,*" I said. "*She always does.*"' Rowan gazed at her adoringly and Clara squirmed.

'She doesn't save it on her own, you know,' Nick murmured.

'Well, no, but—'

'Rowan,' Clara interrupted her. 'Can I go and tell everyone my plan?'

 97

Clara, Nick, and Rowan walked across the field to join Gordon, with Rocky in his pocket, and Bob who were waiting outside the Easter Bunny's big white house.

In the field, bunnies were painting eggs, wrapping chocolate, and some were even making maps of the routes. Clara had to practically yank Nick away from those particular bunnies.

Bob's white house stood proudly with its orange shutters, orange door, and green tiled roof. A white picket fence surrounded its enormous garden which was scattered with beautiful colourful flowers. Tall trees stood proudly bursting with white and pink flowers instead of leaves. Clara had never seen trees like it. They looked like giant ballet skirts or pretty umbrellas!

'They're blossom trees,' Nick whispered to Clara as they walked. She thought these might be her favourite flowers of all.

'From what you've told me,' Clara began once everyone had gathered together, 'there are too many houses for one Easter Bunny to deliver to on his own who has no knowledge of the routes. And there are no bunnies experienced enough to help, right?'

Bob sniffed in response, his whiskers trembling.

'So what we need to do is get organised and get practising,' Clara went on. 'Gordon?' The gnome looked up, surprised that his name had been mentioned. 'I need you to build two train tracks just like the one at your house. You'll be making a kind of production line like the one we've got at the North Pole for some of the toy stations. One bunny will paint one egg one colour, then the train will move on to the next person – sorry, *bunny* – who will do the first line of the pattern. It then moves to the next bunny to do the next colour of the pattern. That way there's no slowing down to wash paint brushes. One bunny, one colour, one pattern. Does that make sense so far? The train will move on with the egg. The same thing will happen with the chocolate stations. The train will be moving constantly making you more efficient – no rushing around back and forth. It also means you'll need fewer bunnies decorating, so some of you could come with me.'

'For what?' asked Bob.

'Why, egg-delivery training of course.' Clara grinned. She was certain that rabbits couldn't be any harder to train than reindeer.

'But I can't build two tracks in two days!' Gordon protested.

'Two days!' wailed Bob, his bottom lip trembling. 'It's only two days until Easter!'

'You'll have to build them quicker than that if we want everything ready on time.' clarified Nick.

'It will be fine.' Clara brushed everyone's concerns aside. 'And Bob can then use the tracks every year to help him. It's brilliant. You're in charge of organising the decorating stations, Nick. Now, let's get cracking! Let's hop to it! Let's—'

'Clara,' groaned Nick. 'No more Easter jokes, please.'

'Don't you mean Easter yolks?' she quipped. Nick shook his head and began to organise things. Clara smiled proudly as everyone busied themselves. *Honestly,* she thought. *What can possibly go wrong?*

CHAPTER TEN

Bunny Training

Gordon was the only one able to communicate with rabbits, but as he was far too busy building the tracks to help, it was up to Clara to get the bunnies to listen to *her*. With her vast experience training reindeer, Clara was sure that this wouldn't be too tricky at all.

The first thing she noticed when training rabbits was just how different they were to reindeer. To begin with, the bunnies kept hopping all over each other, all over Clara, all over the field and, well, all over everything and everyone really (something which her reindeer most definitely never did).

 105

'Bunny up!' she ordered, expecting the bunnies to huddle around her.

They didn't.

'That means come over to me,' Clara explained. Still the bunnies didn't move. Most of them were too busy nibbling on the grass. 'Rabbits!' she called over. 'Here, rabbits – come here!' Clara tapped her legs… and at last all the bunnies hopped over to join her. Clara checked her watch and gulped. They needed to hurry if the bunnies were going to be trained on time.

'First, we're going to practise delivering the eggs.' Clara pointed to a big yellow basket she'd placed at one end of the field. 'Take one of these eggs and one of the maps.' Clara held up the maps that Nick had quickly drawn, which showed various places on the field. 'You

deliver the egg to the place marked on the map and then hop back here for the next egg. I'm going to time you. The first to deliver all five of their eggs wins!' The rabbits stared at her, twitching their noses. 'Okay?' There was still no reaction and Clara wasn't sure if they understood her at all. She could ask Gordon to translate, but as he had two entire train tracks to build, Clara was on her own. 'Ready? Go!' she cheered.

The bunnies raced off and for a brief moment, Clara was filled with hope. All twenty bunnies hopped towards the basket. Unfortunately only two bunnies made it over to Clara – the rest having decided that the grass was much more interesting – and only one of *those* bunnies actually grabbed an egg from the basket.

'Here.' Clara shoved a map at the egg-grabbing bunny, who immediately started chomping down on the paper.

'No!' Clara tried to grab the map. 'Stop eating it, please.' But it was no good. The map was gone.

'Okay, let's try something else.' Clara ran her fingers through her hair.

'Bunny up!'

But the bunnies did nothing. The map-eating, egg-grabbing bunny (whom Clara was pinning her hopes on) was now lying on top of an egg. He began rolling back and forth on his tummy, the egg beneath him, until he started rolling down the hill. Clara stood with her mouth open wide. *Is he snowboarding on an egg?!* Clara watched in shock as some of the bunnies joined with the egg-boarding. Other bunnies began playing catch with the eggs! *Milk and cookies,* thought Clara, *this is a disaster!*

'How's it going?'

Clara swung around to find her brother walking towards her.

'How's it going?' she shrieked. 'How do you think it's going?! They're not listening, Nick! I can't get them to listen!'

'Okay, calm down.'

'Calm down!?' Clara glared at her brother.

'Have you explained *why* they're helping?' he suggested. Clara shook her head. Surely the rabbits already knew why they were helping. 'Come on, Clara.' Nick grinned. 'You need to make one of your rallying speeches.'

Clara crinkled her nose and frowned, annoyed that she hadn't thought of the idea herself. 'Right,

bunny up!' Clara said to the rabbits before remembering that they didn't respond to that. 'Here, bunnies, come here – that's right, here, bunny bunnies.' She patted her legs repeatedly, ignoring Nick's rather unhelpful chuckling. Sure enough, the bunnies were soon sitting on their hind legs in front of her.

'The Easter Bunny – you might know him as Bob – brings joy, and scrummy chocolate, to lots of children,' Clara began. 'Without him – and you – think how disappointed all the children around the world will feel. There'll be no egg hunts.' The bunnies pricked up their ears. 'No decorated eggs, no chocolate eggs.' The bunnies' big eyes drooped and Clara was sure they were about to cry. 'The poor children will be really sad!' One bunny began sobbing at this, tears spurting from its eyes like a sprinkler. *Bunnies sure cry a lot,* thought Clara. 'That's why the Easter Bunny needs you. The children need you – and I know you can do it! But I need you to listen. We'll take it slowly. One step, or hop, at a time!'

The bunnies were silent, just like before, and Clara's heart began to sink. Then one bunny hopped up to the egg-filled basket, looking up at Clara questioningly, its head tilted to one side with one of its ears flopping over.

'Aww,' said Nick.

'Take an egg,' Clara encouraged. 'That's it, good bunny.' The bunny grabbed the egg at Clara's request. 'Now the map – here, take the map… take it, yes! Good

bunny.' Clara held her breath and waited to see what it would do next. Slowly, it hopped over the meadow and delivered an egg to the exact spot marked on the map. *Hurrah! One egg down, only another ninety-nine to go!* Clara checked her watch. *Bee spit and pinecones!* Yes, the bunnies were doing better at training now, but there was only a day and a half before children started waking up, expecting egg hunts. They were never going to get this done on time! Maybe the others were having more success.

'You carry on here, Nick – I'm going to check on Gordon.'

'Clara!' Nick put his hands on his hips. 'You're not the boss, you know. We're a team, remember?'

'I know that, Nick,' Clara reassured her brother although she thought it was quite clear who

the boss was – it was her plan after all. 'And as the important team member that you are, it's really great that you've offered to stay here with the bunnies so I can see how the tracks are progressing. Thanks, Nick!'

Clara raced off before Nick could say anything else. The tracks were bound to be going better than the bunny training, Clara was sure of it.

CHAPTER ELEVEN

Chaos

Clara smiled at the blossom trees as she rounded the corner to Bob's back garden, where the track was being built. She marvelled how a tree that didn't have any Christmas lights or decorations could make her feel so happy. But her delight soon faded when she saw the mess in front of her.

Gordon had managed to build two small round tracks, big enough for all the sections that the bunnies needed. Small stations had been placed in intervals around the track. On one track there was a station for egg dipping the main colour, a station for one colour pattern, another station for another colour pattern, and one station to dry the eggs. There was also a track for chocolate-melting (the bunnies had to be very careful with this part because melting chocolate was hot), with a moulding station to shape the chocolate (one for egg shapes and one for bunny shapes) and a station to wrap the chocolate eggs. Finally, on each track, there was a station for the bunnies to take the finished eggs and place them in beautifully woven baskets. Clara would have said Gordon had done an excellent job, except…

All the stations were empty of bunnies and there were eggs, and bunnies, lying all over the grass. Gordon was sitting with a screwdriver in one of his hands and Rocky huddled into the other, her feathers ruffled. She was tweeting so loudly that Clara could barely hear Gordon murmuring back to her.

Rowan stood on the far side of the field, her arms up in the air as robins flew erratically around her. 'It's okay,' she crooned to the Scouts. 'You're okay.'

Bob was rooted to the spot outside his house, a spatula in his hand, warm liquid chocolate dripping down onto his giant bunny paws and the green grass below. He was staring at the track, his eyes glazed over, his whiskers drooped and his mouth hanging open.

'What in the cookies?' Clara didn't understand what had happened. 'Rowan?' Clara called as she walked over to her. 'What's going on? And what's wrong with the Scouts?' Clara ducked down as robins flew through her hair and flapped their wings furiously. They looked terrified!

'Oh, thank goodness you're here,' Rowan exhaled. 'You'll make it better, Clara. I just know you will.'

'Make what better?' But Rowan didn't have time to reply.

'Oh no, not again!' groaned Gordon.

Clara turned and saw exactly what the problem was: rabbits.

A bunny had hopped into one of the train's carriages. Another bunny into the other. A third bunny had the train remote control in its front paws. The 'on' switch was flicked and the train bunnies were off with a whoosh. More and more bunnies jumped onto the carriages. Faster and faster they flew around the tracks. Some of the rabbits had their hands up in the air whilst yelling, 'Woohoo!' and some held on tight to the sides of the carriage with their paws. The bunnies in the meadow jumped up and down as they watched with glee. It was as if they were on some sort of funfair ride, realised Clara.

'Stop adjusting the speed!' roared Gordon as he stormed over to the bunny with the control.

'They're making it go faster,' explained Rowan.

The bunny with the controls was too fast on his paws for Gordon. He hopped and dodged as the gnome tried to grab it. Eventually Gordon

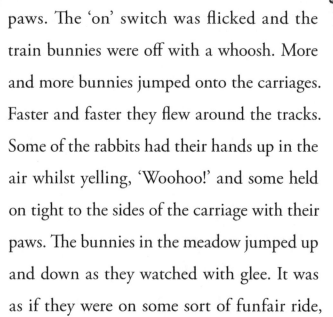

caught the cheeky bunny but he was too clever and threw the controller up high into the air. Another bunny leapt up and caught it and soon Gordon was led on another merry chase. Faster and faster the trains went. The faster it went, the more bunnies bounced on.

Eggs catapulted up high into the air, flinging in all directions. Clara ducked as one narrowly missed her face.

A rabbit whooshed past her on one of the tracks, then another, then another.

'Clara!' Gordon came grumbling over towards her, Rocky poking her head out of his pocket. His face was red and puffy as if he'd been having a snowball fight – or rather a cottontail fight. 'Tell them to stop pressing the speed button. They're going to break it!'

But Gordon's warning came too late. Bits of track began to ping in all directions.

Steam filled the air, followed by a *SCREECH! CLANG! CLANG!*

The trains halted before both toppling over, pulling the track with it – not a single piece remaining in place. Eggs were cracked and jumbled on the ground, bunnies hopped up and down, maps and banners were torn, and baskets had been speared by flying track pieces. Chocolate dripped from trees and all poor Bob could do was stand, spatula still in his paw, staring at the mess in front of him.

'It's ruined!' he wailed. 'Everything's ruined! I'm the worst Easter Bunny ever!' Bob ran off crying back into his house, slamming the door behind him.

'My track!' Gordon stared at the debris.

Nick raced around the corner. 'Clara, what was that noise? Oh no!' He stopped as soon as he saw the mess.

'Nick,' Clara whispered to her brother. 'We're in deep hot chocolate now! How are we going to get all done in time?'

Chapter Twelve

Bunny Training - Again!

Not even a trip on the train could cheer Clara up as they sat around Gordon's table eating a supper of carrot and dandelion pie that evening. No one was talking – no doubt because they were thinking what a failure the day had been, brooded Clara. Only Rocky chirping occasionally broke the silence. Clara could feel the panic rising inside. Blood swirled around her ears, making sounds like the seashell that Dad had given her one birthday.

'Nick, there's so much to do,' Clara fretted as they lay on the sofas, trying to get to sleep that night. 'And I can't get the bunnies to do any of it!'

'Take a breath, Clara,' Nick said softly. 'Little drops, remember.'

Clara nodded. Nick was referring to the last time they'd faced a crisis (just three months ago). Everyone had been relying on them to save Christmas. There'd been a list of jobs (naturally) and everything had gone wrong (much like now). Clara had found the best way to deal with it had been to do each job one step at a time, because little drops make big rivers (or as Clara sometimes thought of it: you can't eat a batch of cookies in one bite, no matter how many times her dad tried). Clara drifted off to sleep whilst formulating another plan in her mind.

First things first, Clara thought as they started afresh the next day. They couldn't deliver the eggs if they had none to deliver, so job one was to make and decorate the eggs. 'Nick, can I leave that with you and Rowan?'

Nick gulped (*he was thinking about what had happened yesterday.*)

'Don't use the track!' Clara quickly added. Nick sighed in relief (*thank notebooks for that!*).

'But can you set up separate stations just like the track had, so that one bunny is doing only one thing?'

'Absolutely.' Nick nodded. 'You can count on me.'

Clara grinned. Despite their bickering, she knew she could always rely on her brother.

'I-I can help too,' stammered Bob, who had silently appeared behind Clara. She turned, surprised to see him. The Easter Bunny hadn't come out of his house since yesterday when he'd bounced off in floods of tears. 'I've… uh… been making chocolate eggs,' the bunny confessed. 'Lots of chocolate eggs actually – it helps me think. And calms me down,' he added with a slow smile. 'I'm here and ready to do whatever you need me to.'

Nick grabbed a clipboard and shoved it at Bob. 'Write down how many eggs you've made so I've got the latest figures.' Bob gulped and nodded, trying to hold a pen between his paws.

'I've made lots of melted chocolate too,' the bunny added. 'Ready for the moulds.'

Nick beamed. 'Excellent.'

Clara watched as a bashful blush crept across the Easter Bunny's cheeks, all the way down to the base of his whiskers.

Satisfied that the egg-making portion of their task was in good hands, Clara turned to face Gordon. 'Can you come with me and the Scouts to help train the bunnies?' she asked hopefully, and was relieved when the gnome nodded.

'Clara,' Nick warned. 'The Scouts have a schedule—'

'It's okay. This classes as training for the Scouts too,' Clara reassured her brother. 'They have to be stealthy and spotted by no one, plus work as a team. All Scout-training schedules will be met, I promise. Right,' she declared. 'Let's get these bunnies trained!'

Clara felt a little sick. She wasn't sure if she could do this. But Rowan had put so much faith in her. Everyone was counting on Clara to make it better. She closed her eyes and thought of all the sad children on Easter morning if they failed… and she knew, no matter what, she was going to keep going and deliver as many eggs as possible. Clara just hoped it would be enough.

The bunnies were a little lively so job two was to calm them down.

'Deep breathing,' Clara announced. It was something she did with any new reindeer before they flew for the first time. 'Breathe in.' Clara showed the rabbits what to do, holding her breath alongside them. 'And breathe out.' The gentle sounds of bunnies breathing floated across the meadow. 'Breathe in,' Clara repeated. 'Breathe out.' The Scouts joined in too, their little red bellies fluttering up and down. Once Clara was satisfied that the bunnies were calm, or at least less bouncy, Clara moved on to job three: practise delivering eggs.

'I want you to bounce.' Gordon translated for her and the bunnies hopped up and down. 'That's it!' Clara cheered. 'Faster!' The little bunnies did as they were told and it was going rather brilliantly, Clara decided. Which meant it was time for the obstacle course.

She put the Scouts into teams of two. Each team had a brightly coloured piece of ribbon with a pouch attached at the middle, which Clara called Easter pockets (she'd got up super-early this morning to make them). A pebble would be placed in every Easter pocket – Clara couldn't risk any Easter eggs – and the Scouts would fly in their pairs, holding each end of the ribbon between their beaks.

Meanwhile, each bunny got lots of pebbles in a pastel-coloured basket. No obstacle course was complete without obstacles, so Clara had placed one of the broken tracks purposefully in the bunnies' way to act like a garden gate. They would have to hop along with their baskets full of pebbles in their paws and find a way through the gate. Then the bunnies would hide the pebble. Obviously the robins could fly over the gate, so they had to hide some of the pebbles in trees as practise for hiding eggs in apartments.

Gordon had explained everything twice – once for the bunnies and once for the Scouts. Clara was grateful that he was there, especially as she supposed it was a little complicated for bunnies that had never done this before.

Clara crossed her fingers and gave the nod to Gordon, who was waiting at the other end of the obstacle course with a stopwatch. He nodded back

and Clara hollered, 'Three, two, one... go!'

The bunnies grabbed their baskets, and Clara placed pebbles in the Easter pockets for the Scouts. She then told each bunny and Scout where they were going according to the map. Not all pebbles made it through the pretend fence unscathed. Some rolled across the meadow, some were trodden into the ground – but all things considered, Clara thought that the bunnies and the Scouts had done a brilliant job. Each journey the animals made was quicker than the one before and Clara began to think that they might just succeed. She might just save Easter.

Chapter Thirteen

Easter Morning

The day was here. Everyone had stayed over at Bob's house to make sure they all had as much sleep as possible for the busy morning ahead. Clara's dreams had been filled with chocolate thanks to the smells that wafted around them, comforting Clara like sunshine on her face.

It was barely two o'clock in the morning but it was time to get up. Clara felt sick, and not just from the copious amounts of chocolate she'd eaten the night before.

'Daffodils!' she exclaimed as she looked outside and saw that the sun hadn't yet risen. Clara hadn't thought to practise egg hiding in the dark – how would everyone cope with this?!

'Morning!' Bob crouched down next to her with a steaming mug of…

Clara inhaled deeply. 'Is that hot chocolate?' She eagerly took hold of the carrot-shaped mug and took a sip. The creamy brown liquid had floating carrot shapes on top that, as they melted, began to ooze more scrumptious chocolate. *Marshmallows and cocoa, this tastes incredible!* thought Clara. *Even better than hot chocolate at the North Pole!* 'Thanks, Bob!'

Bob shuffled his feet. 'No, thank you, Clara Claus.' He blushed and his whiskers twitched. 'Thank you for everything.'

'Can I ask a question?' Something had been bothering Clara ever since she first learnt about it. 'Why is the Easter Bunny afraid of cats?'

 133

Bob jolted and checked around him. 'Is there one here?' he asked in a panic. 'Where is it?'

'No! I was just curious, that's all.' Bob's whiskers were trembling, his ears shaking, and Clara felt terrible that her question had caused so much worry.

'It's a bunny's cottontail,' he confessed. 'It looks like a giant toy to a cat. I can't tell you the amount of times I've had cats launch their claws at my bottom.'

Poor Bob, Clara thought. *Imagine having a cat hanging from your tail!*

Soon everyone gathered in the meadow, baskets and pouches at the ready. Clara and Nova had a sack – although it wasn't red like her dad's but pale green instead. Several enormous wicker baskets filled to the brim with eggs surrounded them and Bob stood in the centre, his paws by his side.

'I just wanted to say… er… thank you to everyone for your help. I've… um… found my first Easter as the Easter Bunny tricky, and… well… um… because of you I…' Bob gulped and his whiskers began to quiver. Clara glanced around at the waiting bunnies and Scouts and knew that this wasn't quite the rallying speech that they all needed. Bob began to sniffle and Clara was sure tears wouldn't be far behind.

'We're going to make every child happy this morning!' Clara's enthusiasm trickled across the meadow. 'And that truly is the best thing.'

'Oh, carrots!' interrupted Bob, checking his pocket watch. 'It's getting late. We only have two and a half hours to deliver the eggs. The sun rises at six o'clock!'

'Right, don't worry, don't panic.' Clara punched her fists in the air. 'Let's deliver Easter!'

And they were off. Clara grabbed a map from Nick and Gordon and she and Nova soared upwards, high over the rooftops and down into the gardens below. Hiding the eggs was fun and Clara relished in finding tricky spots for them. The only trouble was, it took much longer than she'd allowed for. When hiding eggs under flowers and plants, Clara had to be careful not to damage any petals or leaves. When hiding eggs inside pots, Clara had to make sure each egg was gently placed so that it didn't crack. And it was dark, which meant that Clara tripped (quite a lot unfortunately) on hoses that had been left unwound, and spades that were strewn across lawns.

Clara's frustration built as she fell over a forgotten shoe, slowing her down further.

Time was flying by almost as fast as Nova and Clara was beginning to panic. She quickly headed back to Nick to get a fresh batch of eggs.

'We've got a problem,' Nick said, racing to greet her whilst Gordon filled up the sack. 'We're really behind schedule, Clara – you're the first ones back to get more eggs.' He handed Clara his clipboard and all she could do was stare at numbers that didn't make sense as Nick continued, 'We're not going to make it, there's no way! So many children aren't going to get their eggs in time.' Nick looked as if he was going to cry.

Clara nibbled her lip. There was always a way, there had to be... so why couldn't she think

 138

of one? Clara paced back and forth, trying to come up with a solution but knowing that time was running out. It was almost five o'clock in the morning – they only had one hour left. She didn't have time to think! And she didn't know what to do. She had no ideas, no plans, nothing. Everyone was relying on her. They all needed Clara to save the day.

'I don't know what to do,' she admitted in a whisper. Nova nudged her hand and Clara stroked her reindeer, craving the comfort Nova gave. She'd let everyone down. All those children. Tears burned her nose and a lump formed at the back of her throat. Then something caught Clara's eye. A rustling in the trees up ahead. Hope fluttered in Clara's chest like a butterfly in the meadow.

'We need to make our team bigger,' she announced. 'We need team members who can get to all the places the bunnies can't, and quickly.'

Nick pursed his lips, puzzled. 'Where are we going to find more team members?'

Clara pointed up at the tree canopy above her head.

Nick scanned the trees to see what had caught Clara's attention. He frowned at his sister, less convinced. Something was crawling head first, down the tree. It leapt to the ground and scampered across the forest floor.

Squirrels.

CHAPTER FOURTEEN

Super Squirrels

Time was tight – one-hour-left-to-deliver-and-hide-all-the-eggs tight – and what with the all the problems Clara had gone through when trying to communicate with the bunnies the first time around, she asked Gordon to speak to the squirrels to speed things along. He let out a loud screech, forcing Clara and Nick to cover their ears, and sure enough squirrels began to trickle into the meadow.

Gordon barked at the squirrels (actual proper barking, just like dogs did) and the squirrels barked back. This was followed by what Clara could only describe as quacking sounds.

Gordon grunted. The squirrels hissed. It was incredible to watch. And very, very weird. One particularly scrappy squirrel with the bushiest of tails chattered the loudest. Her name was Scamp, Gordon told them, and she was in charge of the scurry (the word for a group of squirrels, as Nick explained to Clara). There was a lot of chattering between Scamp and Gordon and to Clara it sounded a bit like the noise sticky tape being pulled from a roll makes. She hopped from foot to foot, desperate for the squirrels' answer.

Finally, Gordon turned to face Clara and Nick.

'They've agreed to help on one condition. Food. Well, help getting food. Spring is a tricky time of year for squirrels because the nuts they buried in autumn and winter begin to sprout, making them inedible. We gnomes try to do what we can to help, but Scamp says the squirrels have spent most of their time this year scrabbling around, struggling to find something to eat, and they're hungry.'

'I'm sure Bob and the bunnies would be happy to help you once Easter is over,' Clara said to the squirrels as Gordon translated.

The squirrels huddled up into a circle, facing each other, their bushy tails swaying from side to side. Why was it taking so long? Clara tried to ignore Nick checking his watch and clicking his pen repeatedly as they waited for the squirrels to make up their minds. At last Scamp turned and gave Clara a giant thumbs up. Hope surged through her. They might just do this. They might just save Easter.

Clara was worried the squirrels would need training and began to panic because they didn't have any time. But Gordon reassured her that they didn't need it and he continued to bark instructions at their latest team members.

Armed with maps and baskets full of eggs, Clara and Nick watched as the squirrels set off. They bounded from one tree trunk to the next, holding on with their claws, baskets swaying. For a moment Clara thought the eggs would tumble out, but they didn't. Squirrels were seriously amazing.

'What's wrong?' asked Nick as Clara sighed.

'Nothing, it's just… why didn't I think about asking the squirrels before?'

Nick tilted his head (*it wasn't like Clara to look so glum*). 'Not everyone's as perfect as me, Clara,' he replied (*in the most serious tone he could muster*).

Clara stared at her brother. 'What?!' She couldn't believe her ears! Then Nick winked at her and Clara couldn't help but grin. 'You're so annoying.'

'Not as annoying as you,' Nick retorted, smiling back at his sister.

There was no time to waste – the sun was nearly up. She loaded her sack with more eggs and off Clara flew on Nova. As she reached an apartment building, a familiar chattering caught her attention. Clara stood open mouthed as a squirrel catapulted an egg up high in the air and another squirrel leapt out from a tree to catch it. The egg was thrown to a different awaiting squirrel and on it sailed – from squirrel to squirrel and tree to tree. She smiled. Was there anything these squirrels couldn't do?

Clara jumped to the ground as Nova landed and dashed to hide her last eggs. Bunnies were hopping along, baskets in their paws, lifting shrubs and hiding eggs. Clara grinned. They were really rather brilliant too. She turned and saw Scouts with their Easter pockets flying proudly. Squirrels balanced on wires and leapt through the air like reindeer. And the giant Easter Bunny hopped on his hind legs to hide eggs, beaming from one big floppy ear to the next.

The sun had fully risen by the time she'd hidden her final egg. Relieved, Clara and Nova made their way back to the meadow. Clara nibbled her lip as they flew, wondering if everyone had managed to deliver and hide all the eggs on time. One thing Clara did know was that this morning had been an Easter like no other. Despite the early hour, Clara had witnessed animals working together, the fluffiest team in existence, and she was beyond amazed at what they'd achieved.

 147

CHAPTER FIFTEEN

Oodles of Chocolate!

'Well?' Clara asked Nick as she landed in the now empty meadow. She was grateful when Gordon took Nova off to be brushed down and fed. Nerves swirled around Clara's tummy as she waited to hear if they had succeeded or not.

'It all went egg-cellently.' Nick grinned. 'Egg-sactly as planned. You did it.'

Clara felt relief wash over her. '*We* did it, Nick. All of us.'

'Can you believe that four hours ago this field was filled with baskets of eggs?' Nick shook his head. 'Now look at it.'

Clara gazed around at the field. Wild flowers were beginning to open and show their beautiful colours. Excitement prickled Clara's skin as the realisation sunk in. They'd actually done it! They'd saved… Clara's face fell as she spotted something. 'Nick! What's that over there?' Underneath a tree by the woods sat two baskets – one green, one red. Daffodils and dandelions! They'd missed a delivery!

Nick checked his list. (*Those baskets definitely hadn't been there a second ago. He was certain that all the deliveries had been made. He'd checked everything. Twice!*)

Bob hopped out of the woods, grinning from one big floppy bunny ear to the other. He beckoned the children over with his paw. Some bunnies by his feet were jumping jubilantly up

and down and Clara swore she could see some
Scouts with a banner in their beaks. 'It's your
turn now,' Bob said, handing them a basket.
'Time for your Easter egg hunt!'

EGG HUNT
THIS WAY

'Our turn?' Clara didn't know what to say. She looked over at her brother who looked just as surprised as she was, and together they walked into the woods.

Clara gawked. Brightly coloured ribbons were wrapped around tree trunks (squirrels were rushing around with ribbons in their mouths putting up the finishing touches!).

Yellow, pink, and purple bunting hung from trees and from Scouts hovering proudly in the air. Pale green signs had been hammered into the ground. One said: 'Egg Hunt This Way' and another: 'Happy Easter'.

Clara and Nick hopped, skipped, and jumped down the path, searching for eggs (and eating a few along the way). They giggled as they hunted. This was fun! No wonder people loved Easter.

Clara stopped. 'Can you hear music?'

Nick craned his neck. 'I think it's a party!'

Clara raced ahead and squealed as she rounded a corner. 'It's a parade! An Easter parade!'

Bunnies in waistcoats of various shades of pastel colours followed a band of bunny musicians down the path into Bob's garden. They were playing a selection of songs that Clara and Nick had never heard before (being used to Christmas tunes). Squirrels jumped and jived alongside the band wearing an assortment of brightly coloured top hats. (Clara wondered where they'd got the hats from and what sort of special occasion the squirrels usually saved them for.) Bob's garden was scattered with baskets brimming with carrots, and both squirrels and bunnies helped themselves to the fresh supply of food. Bunnies thumped their paws loudly on the ground in celebration as they spotted Clara and Nick.

'About time you two got here,' grumbled a voice beside them. Clara whirled round and saw Gordon, Rocky poking out of his pocket as usual, with Nova at his side. He winked at them and grinned.

Nick strode on towards a chocolate fountain. (*He was eager to dive in – not literally, although it was certainly big enough.*) A bunch of bunnies were basking in the sunshine on the fountain. Chocolate dripped off their fur but they lapped it up and carried on with their warm chocolate dipping. The sweet aroma of decadent chocolate wafted around Nick and he couldn't help himself. Slurping carefully from the side (*he didn't want to sip up any fur*), Nick drank the delicious chocolaty delight.

'Thank you for everything, Clara and Nick Claus,' Bob said, appearing in front of them in a silver sequinned waistcoat and snazzy black bow tie.

'You're very welcome,' Clara replied, her grin growing as Bob handed her a very special chocolate egg. It was carved with her face – and Nick's! – and was mouth-wateringly beautiful. Clara couldn't wait to crack it open.

'You can't eat that!' Nick stopped Clara as she was about to take a massive bite of delicious egg. 'It's got our faces on!'

'What else am I supposed to do with it?' Clara asked.

'We'll give it to Mum,' her brother replied. 'She can freeze it and then it will always remind us of our time here.'

Clara rolled her eyes. Nick's idea was actually lovely but she certainly wasn't going to tell him that.

Eventually the party drew to a close and the bunnies and squirrels drifted off to their

burrows (it had been a long day, after all).
Clara and Nick looked around the meadow
once more. They'd only been here a few days,
but Clara was going to miss the green grass
and the colourful flowers that surrounded
them. She was going to miss the warmth
of the sun and indoor stables and riding on
train tracks. She would even miss training
rabbits. (But she definitely *wasn't* going to
miss bee spit – yuk!)

'It's been fun, hasn't it?' her brother said softly.

Clara nodded. She couldn't speak from
the waves of emotions that washed over her –
because most of all, Clara was going to miss
her new friends.

'Right, you two,' Gordon called as he
walked towards them. Bob trailed behind

him, looking glum. 'Rocky and I expect some letters – and a visit or two wouldn't go amiss either.'

Clara grinned and nodded.

'Well, I'll have to check the schedules.' Nick got out his trusty notebook. 'But I'm sure we can make time.'

 160

'You'd better do, Nick Claus!'

'I was thinking…' Nick's voice sounded a little unsure and Clara wondered what he was about to say. 'It would be nice to have you over to visit us – you, Rocky, Bob and Rowan. As a welcome to the new Easter Bunny.'

Bob burst into tears (again) and stammered out a 'Tha-thank you!' Rowan nodded cheerfully beside him.

'That's a great idea, Nick!' Clara beamed. (She wasn't used to her brother having so many good ideas.)

'You don't need to sound so surprised.' Nick rolled his eyes but Clara could see he was embarrassed – his face had gone as red as a robin's chest.

As they mounted Nova, Clara felt proud of herself once more (*whilst Nick felt a little sick thanks to all the chocolate he'd eaten*). They'd done it. Clara Claus (with a little help from Nick, some super squirrels, bouncing bunnies, and stealthy Scouts) had saved Easter.

Thank chocolate for that.

TURN THE PAGE FOR
MORE EASTER FUN
FROM CLARA, NICK
AND FRIENDS!

JUST LIKE BOB AND HIS BUNNIES, YOU CAN MAKE YOUR OWN BUNTING!

You will need:

- Paper
- Ruler
- Pencil
- Colouring pencils or pens
- Scissors
- Hole punch
- String or ribbon

Instructions

1. Draw a large triangle shape onto a piece of plain paper, using a ruler to keep the edges straight.

2. Making sure the triangle is upside down and the tip is at the bottom, decorate the triangle using either patterns or drawing a picture of a bunny, an Easter basket or even a decorated egg. You might want to decorate both sides.

3. Carefully cut the triangle out – remember that scissors are sharp!

4. Using a hole punch, make a hole at both ends of the top of the triangle. Thread the ribbon or string through the top of the bunting and link with any other triangles you have made.

1.

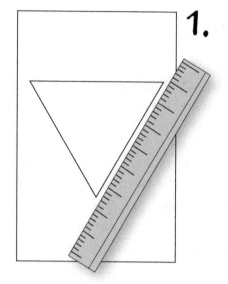

2.

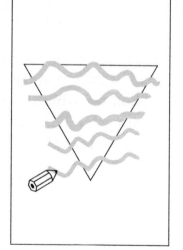

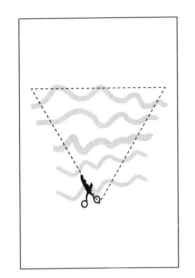

3.

4.

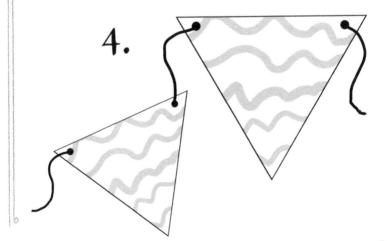

Clara Claus Saves Easter Word Search

Can you help Clara find the missing words?

```
R  O  M  O  R  M  O  S  S  O  L  B
O  I  N  E  G  G  Y  N  G  Y  U  A
W  F  R  N  T  E  K  S  A  B  M  C
A  C  M  H  Y  A  C  L  T  Y  H  M
N  E  E  O  E  N  O  D  R  O  G  H
L  H  D  P  I  N  R  S  C  E  M  E
E  P  A  A  K  E  S  O  L  O  T  V
R  T  R  L  D  I  L  K  A  I  U  N
R  T  A  O  W  A  C  A  R  R  O  T
I  G  P  R  T  R  M  Z  I  C  Y
U  M  Y  E  I  N  D  S  B  N  S  E
Q  E  A  S  T  E  R  E  O  I  N  I
S  D  A  I  Y  N  N  U  B  O  N  D
```

EGG	ROWAN	SCOUT
CHOCOLATE	CARROT	TRAIN
BOB	BUNNY	BASKET
GORDON	BLOSSOM	PARADE
ROCKY	SQUIRREL	EASTER

Clara's favourite chocolate covered pineapple (yum!)

Ingredients

- Pineapple

- Chocolate chips for melting. Clara prefers milk chocolate but you can use dark chocolate or white chocolate if you'd prefer

- Optional cocktail sticks, lollipop sticks or wooden skewers

- Optional White chocolate for drizzling

Instructions

1. Chop up the pineapple. You will need a grownup to help with this because knives are sharp. Clara prefers slices of pineapple, but you can use chunks if it's easier.

2. Cover a baking tray with greaseproof paper or parchment paper and put to one side.

3. Melt the chocolate: Add the chocolate chips to a microwavable bowl and microwave for 30 seconds. Stir the mixture with a wooden spoon. Repeat this process 1-3 times until the chocolate is completely melted.

4. Dip the pineapple into the melted chocolate one by one. Be careful here– melted chocolate is very hot! Clara sometimes uses a spoon to put the chocolate over the fruit instead.

5. Place the dipped pineapple onto the parchment lined tray and pop the tray into the fridge so that the chocolate cools and sets. This may take around one hour.

6. Optional. Drizzle white chocolate over the top and set once more in the fridge.

7. Gently push lollipop stick/cocktail sticks/skewers into the end of the pineapple if you are using them and enjoy the scrummy snack!

Acknowledgements

Wow! Clara Claus Saves Easter is out in the world! Hooray! As always, I would like to thank Pickled Ink and specifically the incredible Helen Boyle who is beyond fantastic. You truly are the best agent out there but also a wonderful person, thank you for everything.

Thanks also to Catherine Coe who is equally brilliant and the best editor around. Thank you to Tiki for being the inspiration behind the mischievous bunnies! Thank you to Jo and Becky, the original Rabbits for the laughs, support, hugs and tears. To the entire class of bunnies, now Robins, keep reading and being the wonderful children you are.

To the team at Tiny Tree, thank you for believing in Clara and in me. To the talented Louise Forshaw, thank you for your beautiful illustrations. To my mum, always. To Mark and Daisy for being with me every step of the way. Thank you, thank you, thank you.

To my family and friends who buy every book I write, I am eternally grateful. Thank you to the readers for your amazing messages of support; I am a very lucky writer!